T0146918

IMPROVING MY *Lie*

Golf Fiction in Verse

DAVE HUTCHINSON

Order this book online at www.trafford.com
or email orders@trafford.com

Most Trafford titles are also available at major online book retailers.

Front cover illustration by Cory Van Ieperen

Printed in the United States of America.

ISBN: 978-1-4907-0639-9 (sc)
ISBN: 978-1-4907-0638-2 (e)

Trafford rev. 07/01/2013

 www.trafford.com

North America & international
toll-free: 1 888 232 4444 (USA & Canada)
fax: 812 355 4082

Author's note: The poem, The Masters 2012—Dear Mr. Fantasy, pays homage to the musician, singer and songwriter Steve Winwood.

"wait for the ricochet"

-Lord, Paice, Gillan, Glover, Blackmore

Improving My Lie is dedicated to those who dig watching good rolls become dirt divers.

Thank you
Ken K. McQueen

Table of Contents

Hutchinson vs. Plimpton

Hole		1	Plimpton	+1	Hutchinson		+1

At the first tee, the Japanese Admirals prepared them for sea
Dispirited and dissolute they were destined for their last hurrah
An eccentric crew that drank its liquor quicker, which made them bicker
No snicker, the ship was Brobdingnagian, no thicker, Tora
It was massive even monstrous, and of course they mostly yelled, "Tora"
And they mostly yelled, "Tora"

Bomber aircrew with a true north wind at their back, walked the tarmac
Single file, soft of step, given a choice they would submit to stay
A crew resigned to fate, it was a sentiment that was innate
A plane they loved to hate, it affected their gait, up up away
The heavy bomber in hues of black with bay doors that fell, away
Bombardiers voiced, "Bombs away"

Yamato cast off low on fuel, on a one-way voyage to duel
Its mission monumental, its mandate, mangle the aorta
Failure was not an option, but keep in mind the chatty coxswain
Bent on destruction, Admirals set course without caution, Tora
Plimpton loosened his lanky limbs and the Admirals yelled, "Tora"
And they mostly yelled, "Tora"

Sports world inferno
Performing under pressure
Grace and dignity

Both wheels retracted on the Lancaster, noted the minister
Custom became cerebral concern because he checked each day
Lancaster's leather-clad crew of seven, headed toward heaven
Take off acceleration forced their expression, up up away
The game began, I took a breath and brought about my takeaway
Plimpton look out, "Bombs away"

Hole	2	Plimpton	+2	Hutchinson	+2

On the second tee box, the Admirals steered clear of charted rocks
The Karpon boilers set to cruise creating a currish sauna
Zigging and loose items went smashing, zagging produced a splashing
Plimpton pondered a fairway bunker while tipping his fedora
Plimpton packed his Pebble Beach yardage book, then tipped his fedora
"Piece of cake," I heard, "Tora"

"Initiative and skill," Bomber Group's motto, all this and ammo
Solo and sitting silent at each station most select to pray
They freeze high above their enemies, yet none sat in their civvies
These sorties call for heavy woollies, not all will come back today
My sand wedge approach lacked any spin, it will not come back today
Should have taken the safe way

Palm trees to flagpoles
Lost a ball on red clay roof
Waves crashing seawall

The Admirals zig-zagged their task force, mockingly staying on course
With hatches battened battle began, cancelled were leaves for Burma
The coxswain capped his sake, sipping later and going banshee
Flares sprayed the blue sky as others had tea, all wishing for karma
With bunkered balls he became the Bogeyman of California
Heard in the din, "Tora"

Navigation was difficult, it determined the end result
Cloud tested their conviction, it can cause carnage and disarray
A break in the cover meant orientation to a marker
Sighting the white marker confirmed what they were after, straightaway
I too took longer over my putt, yes tricky but, straightaway
Hope not all putts are this way

Hole	3	Plimpton	+3	Hutchinson	+5

The Admirals approached the third, all buttoned and neatly tailored
They felt no need to fight fright after they found a massed flotilla
The boiler room bell was tolling, and the mighty ship kept rolling
While veering the coxswain kept steering the Japanese armada
A forced three-wood finding the fairway, he advanced his armada
Positioned to yell, "Tora"

Frigid play cool hand
Country duffer army hack
I am the snowman

A crosswind over the channel, was all the pilot could handle
His hands were hard on each handle when it was heard, "mayday, mayday"
Falling from formation one plane lost power and went spiralling
It was not surprising, but distressing since they were not halfway
As a lefty the dogleg left was leverage before halfway
Hit a lovely fade away

Recognisant planes were still overhead, they followed the spearhead
Counter measures concluded, they continued to Okinawa
There was no hiding, the Yamato's size was easy spying
Shirtless men flitted about sweating, not one resembled Buddha
Confident Plimpton carried on, no need to call upon Buddha
And they mostly yelled, "Tora"

Eyes looked about, they were looking for any sign of a bailout
This sortie lacked a promising start, soon they would enter the fray
Chute fumbling ensued, taking to the silk would be done while shaking
Shaking was common but not normal, all wished for a better day
First four-putt, not repeatable but not fatal on this game day
Not exactly bombs away

Approach putt with speed
Around the world then lip out
No gimme tap in

Hole	4	Plimpton	+4	Hutchinson	+5

On the fourth hole the Admirals perused each minion as a mole
Which peon had palmed off their Pacific course to America?
Yamato's bow came down crashing, crashing then they saw the splashing
Discomfort in the spying, it tempered each man's euphoria
Plimpton paused and pondered, he lacked his earlier euphoria
What is the cure for nausea?

Keeping formation, refocusing on the night operation
Danger of diving into the dank, no pilot dared to downplay
Four propellers screaming and howling, north coast of Europe calling
Training days had them diligently watching the dials on display
Determination and dedication was their outward display
A seven in tight, hurray

Recognisance aircraft released a flare that continued to glare
Admirals requested its escorts to be ready to rumba
While still veering, the coxswain kept sipping, then zigging and zagging
Engineers' shirts were ripping, retrofitting to a bandana
Shirtless men singing, the ship a splashing, each wore their bandana
Chorus was "Tora, Tora"

Rustic wooden fence
Golden Bear in Golden years
Par dust to par dust

This was the second wave, most Nazi kills were on the second wave
Seven hundred bombers with bomb bays bulging emptying the taxiway
The enormous attacking group increased their chance for surviving
By far marshalling was the safest part of the German airway
My two-putt parlayed to par allowing me to clear my airway
Bogeyman be gone, hurray

Hole	5	Plimpton	+5	Hutchinson	+6

Japanese surface special attack force did not readjust course
Instead the seaman got all secretive in code from Asia
There was transmitting and receiving before radio jamming
Bungo Strait navigating exposing the plan, Okinawa
Submarines a-skulking, splashing all the way to Okinawa
And they mostly yelled, "Tora"

The distinctive greenhouse cockpit, did not help from being frostbit
Neither could it stop bird strikes or bullets, even a ricochet
Elevating and elevating until their extreme ceiling
First numbness then freezing, it was not much warmer in the bomb bay
Feet freezing with boots frozen to the floor even in the bomb bay
Move your feet when bombs away

Tsunami ball strike
Tuning forks quell wave for par
Bent grass grows again

Japanese surface special attack force, itched for a fight of course
Buoyancy preparedness purged flammables, beds were believed extra
Sleeping on the floor gave them a raw, red, rash, soon they were scratching
Plimpton's bag had light packing, packing just a faded fedora
The west wind was picking up, whipping at his faded fedora
Oh his faded fedora

Lambskin lining over a heated suit, then they sat on their chute
Standard issue gear had a shiny sheen, still they froze night or day
The Lancaster was lacking, lacking some cabin pressurising
This par I was choking, choking on a chip from too far away
The pressure of performing was letting the game pilfer away
Par threes were needed today

Hole	6	Plimpton	+7	Hutchinson	+8

Air search radar operator grumped when he saw, he was in awe
Sharpening his screen, sipping some sake, words were stuck in his craw
No doubting his round display, no doubting the ominous massing
With words passing they saw massing between them and Okinawa
Almost three hundred Hellcats dead ahead, holding Okinawa
And they mostly yelled, "Tora"

Rehearse putting stroke
Rolls that become dirt divers
Just a bit lippy

Turbulence kept the upper gunner permanently off balance
Swinging on a canvas sling he stared at the sinister bomb bay
His stomach was churning while he closed his eyes to stop the blurring
Starring down the ball, my pulled drive came back from over Carmel Bay
A left-handed swing, leaving Plimpton aghast, over Carmel Bay
Bomb sights in order today

The operator grumped again, the mass split doubling the pain
The wind brought the Admirals' attention back to their armada
Splashing into the unknown, the operator began to moan
Bogeyman as he is known, in Pebble Beach California
Plimpton's first poke planed straight into the ocean off California
Plimpton tipped his fedora

The mid-upper gunner was new, barely known to the aircrew
Navigator drew his curtain, checked the complaint without delay
Decompression sickness was frightening, it could lead to dying
Navigator began switching, switching his mask without delay
After my own double I wanted to move on without delay
Move forward, keep ball in play

Low tide high surf roll
Undulating rock and roll
Pull the pin and dive

Hole	7	Plimpton	+8	Hutchinson	+10

Staring into the vast distance imagining the resistance
Admirals were devising the details of the their defense dogma
Last minute scheming by imperial naval engineering
From the bridge decking they admired the vast panorama
Yamato's gold lettering glittering, in the panorama
Salt spray was the aroma

The Lancaster began buffeting and the aircrew feared icing
Wing watching and wishing on weather the was order of the day
Wing ice glazing when flying so high, could drop them from the
    night sky
Each manned a window nearby, an enemy was in the airway
A clumsy choice, a high-lofted club, it ballooned in the airway
My shot was up, up, away

The Admirals viewed the horizon and considered each option
One hundred and sixty-two anti-aircraft guns and a mantra
They were expecting a naval battle but got an air battle
The world's largest battle vessel had no air support, Tora
Coxswain raised his cup and concentrated on the chorus, Tora
And they mostly yelled, "Tora"

Final round despair
Unable to mount a charge
Coast to coast washout

Flying through clouds with small liquid droplets, forming ice deposits
Each crew member cheered the cloud break, one less enemy was fair play
Plan was for scoring on par threes, a plan that could quickly deepfreeze
Slick greens resulted in three-putting, putting could ruin my day
Things could be worse, what I feared most was the snowman, please
    not today
Snowman, please, please stay away

Hole	8	Plimpton	+9	Hutchinson	+11

The radar operator rose from his chair and began to stare
With a breath he buttoned his blazer and brought out his camera
Standing before the emperor's framed portrait, standing while filming
Filming, filming a bridge deck all bowing toward Okinawa
Shipshape, soldiery and splashing, all the way to Okinawa
Plimpton tipped his fedora

The wing spar made a shudder that caused the mid-gunner to stutter
A violent drop into a void vanquished all calm today
The eighth hole chasm was frightening, I felt my hands tightening
With all my thinking my chances kept shrinking, down at Monterey
My approach an unintended slice worked nice, down at Monterey
Crazy left carry, safe play

Par five back tee box
Dimples on the horizon
A bird is calling

Plimpton's waggle made me think his admirals were being boastful
A shimmy here and an anti-shank there, direct from Asia
A walk away followed by more twitching was exasperating
Admirals firing a long arching salvo to add drama
Bogeyman bagged his bogey with ball striking that had high drama
And they mostly yelled, "Tora"

The mid-gunner with eyes closed, mind afar, placed both hands on
     the spar
He wished the support structure long service as it crossed the bomb bay
Pilot was eyeing, eyeing oxygen that kept them from dying
Navigator was pulling, pulling curtains to keep light away
My top-tier putt rolled downhill, I tried to turn my eyes away
Rolling down at Monterey

Hole	9	Plimpton	+10	Hutchinson	+12

They blathered under binoculars about their naval stragglers
A destroyer escort was estranged exposing the armada
The group was zigging and zagging while the destroyer was lagging
The Admirals increased their splashing and started a fresh mantra
Tempers on a tangent, "Tora, Tora, Tora" the fresh mantra
Would they survive this drama?

As Seen on TV
Repeatable silken swing
Bring club head to square

East of a beach called Juno, the French coast was now a near shadow
A wired suit stepped in stiff of limb to see the striking display
He was pointing, pointing out the canopy, his mask was muffling
"You see they have started their banking, at the turn it is halfway"
My shape off the tee was a steep sidehill lie, the pin was halfway
Bombardiers voiced, "Bombs away"

The escort was under attack, the Yamato could not turn back
A bombardment began with the ruin burned into their retina
Billowing smoke clouds became belated death flowers by blooming
Spiritual shielding began, with a toast to Okinawa
Battle brave to the end, splashing all the way to Okinawa
Plimpton tipped his fedora

He stared out of the astrodome during the bank looking for home
An interlude from reading his radio and radar array
Radio use was fleeting, the enemy sought his signalling
With good timing he would be transmitting, German on the airway
I stole a look at Plimpton wanting to cheat my lie, I daresay
Did not turn to my dismay

Looking over cliff
Depth charge putt locked and loaded
Top of lip is fine

Hole	10	Plimpton	+11	Hutchinson	+15

Gracing Yamato's bow was a glittering gold crest on its prow
The circular chrysanthemum characterised best in its class
Dignity, duty, diligence were traits depicting her essence
Filled with ordinance, no mistake she had a certain gravitas
One-putting with no fist pump, a man of a certain gravitas
The regal Plimpton oozed class

The pilot gave his knee a spank soon after he finished the bank
Anti-aircraft artillery would soon attack in this airway
Past experience had them all knowing, knowing the exploding
Nervousness set in knowing of the deafening in this airway
Putting down a severe slope like slipping a snare on my airway
Snowman, please, please stay away

Plimpton stood on the fringe, holding his short pencil like a syringe
He worked his scorecard then stared at the slope like some salty
     seamen
"Like putting down the wall of a tsunami," he said quite softly
He advanced his tally, as if setting a course for his helmsmen
One-putting then plotting and preparing a course for his helmsmen
Plimpton pushed his lead, again

Poa Annua bloom
See the turn through the slow down
AM to PM

My bomber crew all looked down at the landform, waiting for the storm
They stared down into the face of danger, this was not a cliché
Pilot was eyeing, eyeing altitude that kept them from dying
My putt blew the distant hole rolling, rolling down at Monterey
Oh these blooming Poa Annua greens, rolling down at Monterey
"Man Alive, fast greens today!"

Hole	11	Plimpton	+14	Hutchinson	+16

Grumman Hellcat's appeared first, an American plan well-rehearsed
Avenger airplanes added to the swarm over the armada
Yamato's great guns were training on the air mass that was hatching
Curtiss Helldiver's last in joining, like insects from a larva
The sky over the South China Sea, like insects from a larva
On the bridge they yelled, "Tora"

Looking like drops of spilled paint, dark blotches formed, all
    airplanes be warned
Anti-aircraft artillery shot flak at the midnight airway
At first it was paint splattering, then it came, an ear-shattering
They began dropping, dropping metalized paper in the airway
Plimpton's approach entered a bunker, it had sliced in the airway
"Pebble Beach is now in play"

Take the advantage
Dogleg wind natural slice
Modest shot to shape

Plimpton shot me a glance, as he looked for the errant balls entrance
"Got me a fried egg Davey boy, laughter will run your mascara"
A mighty sand blasting, over the green to the next beach landing
Bunker to bunker he went talking, talking to the barranca
No doubt he admonished his Admirals over the barranca
And they mostly yelled, "Tora"

The bomber force had the ground radar out-foxed, leaving them flummoxed
Aluminum foil sabotaged attempts to stop the foray
All the force got was the shock wave pounding, direct hits were missing
Manual dropping was exhausting, as they crowded the hatchway
Each plane the same, bundles and bundles of foil down the hatchway
Bombardiers voiced, "Bombs away"

Hole	12	Plimpton	+15	Hutchinson	+17

The radio operator yelled, "Tora," then made a rumour
The chatty coxswain choreographed a few steps of the cha-cha
The radar operator kept sipping, but never stopped searching
Engineers began plugging, plugging their ears with their bandana
Admirals actions were animated, each waved their bandana
And they mostly yelled, "Tora"

Beaver pelt divots
Crafted into bacon strips
The sunset years swing

General orders came, all seven hundred airplanes did the same
A two hundred mile mass full of malice bent on a melee
They would ration the metalized paper, it would be used later
The German skies would get much meaner upon entering the fray
Flak round ended providing respite before entering the fray
Bombardiers voiced, "Bombs away"

I watched Plimpton go back to his bag, he then checked eleven's flag
Wanting to let him know I was watching I mentioned the vista
"Keep it below the trees if it's blowing, miss short or its beaching"
Plimpton winced at the word beaching, but hit the green with high drama
Plimpton's putts reclaimed his status of Bogeyman with high drama
Plimpton tipped his fedora

Felt bad giving him the gears but I was a few strokes in arrears
There was a growing desperation to my game, I felt decay
The course, a 145 slope rating, it showed in my putting
Plimpton's putting was unnerving, he put on a dandy display
His Admirals with their pocket puffs, put on a dandy display
Need to make a move today

Stroke play victory
Resort course seascape setting
Read break and get paid

Hole	13	Plimpton	+17	Hutchinson	+18

The Admirals paced all decks, scanning for the USS Essex
No aircraft carrier could be sighted in the panorama
Ship to ship warring was the battle plan they had been preparing
Looking and worrying, splashing all the way to Okinawa
Ship to air was the fare, splashing all the way to Okinawa
Plimpton tipped his fedora

Flying in a staggered formation there was slim hope for salvation
Interlocking support soothed some and saved others from going astray
Flying tight was a plan, they then agreed to return to a man
One station one man, this too was a plan not to stray from today
Slick scoring surface but so far so good, I may take him today
Keep it tight, my plan today

From the chart table, Admirals made noise that could have been naval
There was humming, hawing and hacking, or it could have been asthma
Discussion of the battle was interrupted by a kettle
They showed their mettle with a tea leaf from the edge of East Asia
Plimpton's read required leaf interpretation from East Asia
Wrong read should have drank Kava

Pebbles on the beach
Ocean glare hides Minke whales
Edge of cliff tee box

Pulled my approach right, left with another forty-foot downhill fight
My bombardier pulled his prone position up in the canopy
Facedown the bombardier was laying, nerve racking, not relaxing
Checking the harsh slope while kneeling, I could see the break clear as day
Break a big beautiful arc, "Whiz-bang Davey, shot of the day"
Bombardiers voiced, "Bombs away"

Hole	14	Plimpton	20	Hutchinson	20

Klaxon replaced all song, prepared for anything that could go wrong
Defence designs had dutiful destroyers circling Yamato
Yamato continued splashing, as destroyers began dashing
"Toughest par five in all of golfing," he said, with some bravado
He played to my doubt and despair, delivered with some bravado
Oh please, pass me a bromo

A Junkers JU88 entered the mass, intent to harass
After radioing his altitude he let the ammo spray
My Lancaster a victim of his strafing, it was nerve racking
He was seen leaving after the strafing, the crew began to pray
Junker's mission finding altitude for flak, crew began to pray
Flak coming to their airway

Horseshoeing the cup
Wild balls need to be set free
Three to get ready

From oil cans engineers had their final sake, just tacky
Plimpton's penchant for pomposity was game, but tough to swallow
I think he felt this hole was his for winning, and mine for folding
"This Davey Boy is where your dreams of paring die," such bravado
I watched his chip crawl back to his feet, so ended the bravado
Oh Bogeyman, what a show

There was no intercom chatter and dropped foil did not matter
Guns pointing on the Junkers last position, the pause, torture
With Lancaster's in such a large grouping, no room left for moving
Triple A began blind firing, time to control your terror
The box barrage was well beyond bleak, time to control your terror
Each had never been braver

Hole	15	Plimpton	21	Hutchinson	21

The Hellcats were first to pounce, strafing those manning the anti-
    aircraft mounts
Response was short fuse beehive shells in a protective umbrella
Helldiver bombers began the bombing, all decks took a pounding
One boiler room began flooding, flooding which caused a great trauma
USS Hornet torpedo planes plan, to cause port side trauma
And they mostly yelled, "Tora"

Snow back to snowcap
Coast to coast telephone call
Meandering roll

The flak came to a sudden stop, the crew had concern for one prop
Barrage box brute power took one engine but no life on this day
The fuselage had holes from floor to ceiling leaving them quaking
End of flak meant more fighting, Luftwaffe would be in the airway
Messerschmitt 110 their might in the night would be in the airway
Bombardiers voiced, "Bombs away"

Plimpton was anything but serene as my approach hit the green
Serious but still posing after each shot in California
After his posing, he let the shaft through his hands with a sliding
Homage to pros touring, mostly for those wearing a fedora
"A titular test it's become," he said, tipping his fedora
Oh that faded fedora

My test was at that moment, I could not contain my excitement
I surmised some sputter in the silhouette against Carmel Bay
The game was turning, since being down four at hole ten this morning
"George I am over the moon at being tied," down at Monterey
"My advantage since I've read your book on golf down at Monterey"
Bogeyman, it's not your day

Leaking on the low side
A side door invitation
Roll in and party

Hole		16	Plimpton		22	Hutchinson		24

For the second Yamato attack, the assault did not hold back
Once again torpedoes found their target causing port side trauma
Wave upon wave of dive bombing brought about uncontrolled flooding
With her loopy listing, there would be no striking a vendetta
Stuck on starboard there would be no steering, toward a vendetta
And they mostly yelled, "Tora"

The German might in the night had the Lancaster in his gun sight
The upper gunner fired first lighting him up in a flambé
A second Messerschmitt performed a banking before firing
A hail of fire sent him smoking as he exited the fray
Bundles of foil confused many more from entering the fray
And the gunners blazed away

"Not heard a whizzer in-flight since I last judged a fireworks night"
My fairway metal-wood a warhead over Plimpton's fedora
"Sorry George a wicked topping followed by a wicked slicing"
I was fuming, I got to my ball faster than any cheetah
Wicked lie needing a wangle with risk of being a cheetah
I, I think I heard "Tora"

Pebble Beach Maxim
Never lie above the hole
A flatstick horror

I had just pulled even, to lose a stroke would have been pure poison
I had to wangle my way to a better spot on the fairway
Gave my ball a watering, then called for a risk-reward ruling
George said, "Damn sprinkling, you must take a drop, it's the only
    fair play"
I took a waggle at my wangle then wrenched the ball out of play
No reward to my dismay

Hole		17	Plimpton		23	Hutchinson		26

The Admirals remained upbeat, even in the face of defeat
Admirals led a boisterous round of "Tora, Tora, Tora"
Yamato may have been listing but its crazed crew was still chanting
"All fire!" "Even the girandola?" "Hold the girandola!"
Yamato scorched the South China Sea sky sans the girandola
And they mostly yelled, "Tora"

Intercom was all chatter once bomb doors opened with a clatter
Seven hundred statically charged voices crackled, bombs away
Operators began squawking German just to be deceiving
A dastardly deception, leading to my Pebble Beach doomsday
Fiery trails of Pathfinders flares framing a German doomsday
Bombardiers voiced, "Bombs away"

Monterey Cypress
Century through century
Sea spray to stone dust

Seven blasts at a short clip, one long blast, call to abandon ship
Port side attack caused an inexorable roll toward Asia
Despite rocking, Coxswain saved Emperors portrait before rolling
Yamato lay smouldering, about to be lost to the aqua
Plimpton in a two club wind lost his fedora, to the aqua
Oh his faded fedora

Since engine one had been shot-up the Lancaster strained to keep up
Luftwaffe focused on the straggler flying back to the UK
Hydraulic turrets were rotating and sighting then dogfighting
Luftwaffe gave them a hammering, forcing a call of mayday
Through smoke and flames the crew took to the silk, after calling mayday
Caterpillar club relay

| Hole | 18 | Plimpton | 28 | Hutchinson | 28 |

Yamato's symbolic might was coming to an end in this fight
Main magazines hot as lava imploded in a chimera
The chatty coxswain now life boating, watched the mushroom cloud
    forming
Yamato stopped all splashing in a cloud seen in Okinawa
Slipping into the sea, she never made it to Okinawa
Coxswain gave last chant, "Tora"

Pebble trees of lore
The Lone, Ostrich, Ghost and Witch
Spindly, bleached or dead

I looked down eighteen's seawall with chagrin, then thought of Hale
    Irwin
Trailing The Bing Crosby he birdied by keeping the ball in play
I too was trailing, but all I saw was my ocean side slicing
"George I may be dreaming, dreaming of a Hale Irwin ricochet"
"Don't channel his massacre at Wing Foot over the ricochet"
Stay out of the surf today

With a three shot lead, Plimpton swung his old-school driver at high
    speed
A breeze patted his fine hair while Plimpton pitched to a barranca
I stood watching, as his lanky frame settled its sandy footing
Grim viewing, swing to swing, then good grief, good night and sayonara
From the bunker he picked up, "Great game Davey Boy, sayonara"
Hands shook ending the drama

Plimpton's score took off like a rocket, once he chose, ball in pocket
He paid the price rather than pander to a bunker on this day
My mind was reeling, the Van de Velde-sque moment disbelieving
A paragon of virtues being tested, down in Monterey
I shook his hand, "Yes George, it's been a great game down in Monterey"
Saw his hat in the sea spray

The End

Stunted stooped show piece
Guy wires for life support
Will resuscitate

Hole	1	2	3	4	5	6	7	8	9	out	in	total
Black	380	502	404	331	195	523	109	428	505	3,377	3,663	7,040
Par	4	5	4	4	3	5	3	4	4			
Plimpton	5	6	5	5	4	7	4	5	5	46		
Hutchinson	5	6	7	4	4	7	5	5	5	48		

Hole	10	11	12	13	14	15	16	17	18	out	in	total
Black	495	390	202	445	580	397	403	208	543	3,377	3,663	7,040
Par	4	4	3	4	5	4	4	3	5			
Plimpton	5	7	4	6	8	5	5	4	10	46	54	100
Hutchinson	7	5	4	5	7	5	7	5	7	48	52	100

Quarry quilted aid
A stone's throw from the forest
Skeleton icon

Children's Miracle Network Hospitals Classic 2012— The Rookie

Rookie Charlie Beljan won the PGA's year-end event this week
He did so despite being hospitalized on day two for feeling weak
The rookie lay prone on the 18th with a shortness of breath
The gallery thought the worst: Was the day two leader near death?

The rookie signed his golf score then an ambulance took him away
After an overnight hospital stay he laced them back up the next day
The rookie's weekend rounds brought about plenty of drama
Panic attacks aren't scheduled, I scrutinized for signs of neural trauma

If I were a rookie I could totally see me having a spiked heart rate
Watching Ai Miyazato's silky smooth swing hit the ball straight
If I were a rookie I could totally see me having numbness in my arm
Watching Michelle Wie's power and grace work like a charm

If I were a rookie I could totally see me having a churning stomach
Watching Tiger watch me watching my ball hitting some schmuck
Of course me being a tour rookie would take a whole lotta flim-flam
But thanks to the rookie I now know why I have never entered a pro-am

Bogey no option
Muscle back attack pulled from bag
Replant all divots

Crowne Plaza Invitational at Colonial 2012— Zach Johnson, a Reminder

Two strokes for simply forgetting
Forgetting your ball's original setting
This penalty at the Colonial
It can be fixed by being managerial

You need a new reminder service
To rely on your caddie makes me nervous
Tying a string to your finger may work
But this would draw a competitor's smirk

You need a reminder with drama and flare
A reminder that gives your competitor a scare
A reminder that oozes confidence and charm
It should invoke victory not cause alarm

I suggest a reminder that fits in your bag
When you bring it out it sets tongues a wag
Remember to shoot your cuffs this isn't a gadget
I suggest your reminder be your green jacket

Stimp value in seed
Mark lift assess and drain
It's a numbers game

Farmers Insurance Open 2012—
18ᵗʰ Triple Bogey Breakdown

Kyle Stanley's 72ⁿᵈ finishing hole breakdown
I'm sure made Jean Van de Velde frown
Both are now known for their infamy
Both had triple bogey's that cost them dearly

Stanley's win seemed secure
A four-shot lead is considered safe on this tour
A green's fringe that was shaven
Led to his immolation

I drifted from one snowman to another
The balls backspin made my heart flutter
It rolled down the slope leaving me all out of sorts
I thought of Vinko Bogataj and Wide World of Sports

Like Vinko from the sports show opening montage
I saw a slipping and spinning horror that was no mirage
For Stanley the loss of victory was not yet complete
There was a three-putt then a lost playoff, oh the agony of defeat

The new math posted
Handicapper sandbagger
Fog by any other name

Greenbrier Classic 2012—
Steve Stricker's Caddie

Steve Stricker has his wife on the bag this week
Believe me it's not so the PGA can look oh-so-chic
Nicki is replacing Jimi, his regular caddie
Of course it's an upgrade, Nicki is not at all shabby

Believe me this is not style over substance
Even though Nicki wears Steve's favourite fragrance
Nicki has carried in the past, she's not been miscast
She's there for a reason, that's the forecast

Sure she will get good pocket money
But I believe she prefers to stand next to her honey
All this caddying has nothing to do with nostalgia
It's all about a diva and doing the cha-cha

You see Steve has Tiger in his pairing
And Ellen's friend is there to stop any sharing
Tiger beware when she reaches for the nine-iron
You won't be hearing "fore" from this blonde siren

Gallery corralled
Marshals arm to arm in rough
Let the big dog eat

Kraft Nabisco Championship 2012—The Hutchinson Commission

I was asked if an anchored putter would have helped I.K. Kim
So I viewed her missed putt with same zeal as the Zapruder film
A nominal fourteen inches coming back for her first major
It put her in the company of Sanders and Hoch for failure

The Hutchinson Commission gave the first putt some thought
Like the Zapruder film the key was in the first missed shot
For a previous LPGA winner she seemed to be far too stressed
I saw it as a factor in her not being able to close the contest

Frame analysis then showed the shadows as a major factor
At this point there was no benefit to using a putting anchor
Kim was not of conscious mind as she stepped over the putt
She relied on years of rote practice and a feeling from her gut

Combining shadows with stress she could not see the line
Unconscious stroking is not enough, it's one half of the design
Commission findings, the inability to find the line is to blame
Putter choice is irrelevant the result would have been the same

Provisional ball
Hot shot unseen try again
Burned stroke and distance

LPGA Canadian Open 2012—
"Close Counts Only in Horseshoes and Hand Grenades"

Growing up I always considered the Canadian sporting ethos
In America they flat out won while we were happy to come close
In America they charged hard and were the front runners
While in the Great White North we would gently nudge shoulders

Close didn't fit their baseball as it did for horseshoes or a hand grenade
Comparatively our curling with its closest rock was a scoring charade
In America they knew how to run up the score
While in the Great White North we were satisfied with just a bit more

Growing up Canadian Football scoring always left me befuddled
Winning by missing a field goal is a concept the league fumbled
My neighbours to the south have a crystalline notion of any endgame
My neighbours on the street make the claim but its close, just not the same

This week the Canadian sporting ethos extended a figurative hand
Winner amateur Lydia Ko forfeited her prize money as preplanned
A pro-am condition that second-place Inbee Park received in fair play
That it happened in Canada is fitting I say

Shine shoes sip water
Invite me I'm standing near
Cowbell sounds all clear

Memorial Tournament 2012
Finest Shot

The Jack Nicklaus-hosted Memorial Tournament produced a very
  fine shot
Tiger's 49—foot flop shot it was not
Don't get me wrong holing out with a sixty-degree wedge is a thing
  of beauty
It's just that another shot caught my fancy

Yes the flop shot had drama and flare
It also had timing as it tied the game and begot Sabbatini's despair
And who could deny that the birdie had power and punch?
It contributed to Fowler's twelve-over yes Tiger had him for lunch

Some say Tiger has perfected the flop to show the logo before it dropped
All I know is that the roll was slow and didn't hit the flagstick before
  it stopped
I must admit I admire the juxtaposition of the full swing and trickling ball
But on this day the shot that I held in the highest regard was sentimental

The Memorial's finest shot was Tiger's birdie putt on 18 to win
It's the one that gave me the biggest grin
The dude in red pointed his putter Nicklaus-style for the world to view
Tiger, giving Jack his due, the tribute looked good on you.

Storm is rolling in
Crackling charge down the back nine
Eagle ace lights out

PGA Championship 2012—
What I See

Mcllroy wins PGA major by eight strokes
And it's surprising what images that evokes
I saw a record for margin of victory
I see a future that knows no boundary

Mcllroy at twenty-three has won two majors
Punctuating each with record scores
I saw world's # 1 whose exploits are becoming legion
I see the emergence of a UK lion

Mcllroy's majors have displayed his dominance
Stroke play is a showcase for his brilliance
I saw his hat curtail his locks like a chicane
I see a thick flowing lion's mane

Mcllroy wore a red shirt on the PGA's final day
I saw his choice of colour as having plenty to say
I see a Tiger vs. Lion showdown ahead
I also see plenty of red

Tee box putter blues
Rain drops ball hops Baker's view
Horseshoes and birdies

Phoenix Open 2012—Winter Golf

The Phoenix Open had a cold snap
Spencer Levin went colder than an icecap
He was the day three leader
Day four he stepped into the freezer

It is good in theory
A desert date in February
I'm sure it has good data
It's hard to make snow in Arizona

Total attendance over a half million
Not one wearing a mitten
Levin dropped six with nary a cheer
In the land of sun and beer

Conditions are more than they appear
Problem is the time of year
Winter can make you suffer
From seasoned player to duffer

Club head east of tub
I feel the heat show me how
Would you glue me good

Ryder Cup 2012—
The Eastern Slant

Rory Mcllory did not consider his time zone for his match
It was a tee sheet detail that he failed to catch
Eastern zone needed to be adjusted to the Central zone
Back in the UK it has just one zone, time is well known

With eleven minutes away from forfeiture
Rory pulled up under the escort of a State Trooper
It was a midday mad dash to play in the Medinah dirt
If you are to take on Jack's record you will need to convert

Sharpen your math skills and address this eastern bias
North America is East Coast-centric with all its big business
It is most visible in schedules made for TV
But it is also in politics and I believe geography

In North America not only time travels from east to west
When putting I say consider this on your next five-foot test
The break does not need the high function analysis of a savant
As a UK transplant, you must consider the eastern slant

Do not leave it short
Seismic knee knocker for win
Sink and pump for show

The Masters 2012—
Dear Mr. Fantasy

Dear Mr. Fantasy shape us a shot
Something to make us happy
Do anything, demonstrate your forethought
Pick a club, play the wind, just make it snappy

Dear Mr. Fantasy pick out your pink club
Something to make us all happy
This arc of the driver is your paystub
Pick a club, play the wind, just make it snappy

Dear Mr. Fantasy just love your white garb
Something to make us all happy
Hook it off that pine, or through a deep woods barb
Pick a club, play the wind, just make it snappy

Dear Mr. Fantasy show us something epic
Something to make us all happy
Do anything, even play in all that traffic
Pick a club, play the wind, just make it snappy

Wormburner off tee
Three hundred yards to sand
Spray and rake for par

The McGladrey Classic 2012—
Nicknames

The McGladrey winner has something I fancy
Tommy "Two Gloves" Gainey has a nickname that I envy
I would love one, something homespun
But nicknames are given, they are not taken

I need something creative from my foursome
I want a golf nickname that is awesome
My initials do not add up to something stellar
Not like Frank Urban aka "Fuzzy" Zoeller

I do not have a physical trait like Ernie Els, "Big Easy"
Nor do I have "Merry Mex" aka Lee Trevino's personality
I do not have a playing style like Couples' "Boom Boom"
And metaphors like Hogan's "Hawk" are not about to bloom

But I have earned one, if someone would just catch on
I am notorious for missing putts that are dead-on
If it was up to me, I'd have a nickname that is proven
On the green call me "Gimme" and call me often

Playing all year round
Rooster tails on each fairway
Local winter rules

The Open 2012, Tell Me I'm Wrong . . .

"I have won 145 times . . ." said caddie Steve Williams
At the Bridgestone invitational and heard by millions
". . . and that is the best win of my life,"
A quote causing his prince Adam Scott much strife

I'd like to give the big looper the benefit of the doubt
Sure it sounds sinfully selfish and he comes across as a lout
I'm sure he places a value on his playing partner, he's not naive
Don't worry PGA win leader Sam Snead is not rolling in his grave

Professional golf is a collaborative practice with plenty at stake
His comments, after recently being fired, were full of heartache
Stevie has been in this teamwork culture for over thirty years
During that time he has been a leader amongst his small house peers

At the Open's 72nd hole the decision was anything but benign
Stevie and Adam both chose three-wood over driver with the title on the line
Just in case Stevie tells me I'm wrong and gives me the crisscross
My sympathies on your loss.

Hard fairways fast greens
Coyote trot bump and run
Golf course management

The Players 2012—Kevin Na Should Get a New Sponsor

What exactly is Kevin Na's issue?
His pre-shot routine begs for a rescue
If you listen to his peers
They will say it's all between his ears

Could it be as most would say, OCD?
I do see disorder but mostly I see symmetry
There is no doubt he struggles for a cure
But is it OCD? I am not sure

Could it be the result of a swing that has changed
All that practice and he's become deranged
Gallery taunts of "pull the trigger," rot at his brain
But from where I stand his swing is on plane

Kevin Na needs a new sponsor
The goddess of victory aces any doctor
He needs to embrace her virtues, not those of a fidget
He needs to live the life, a Nike life, "Just Do It"

Struck square on the screws
Willow tree bumper guard rail
Bagging your tree wood

US Open 2012—Golf World War

When is long enough, long enough?
Olympic hole 16 is now 670 yards, that's tough
PGA wanted par five that plays to greens in regulation
Players wanted that birdie sensation

PGA wants to test shot-making skill
Players want to test Bomber Phil
PGA wants toughest test par five at its core
Players want an easy score

Equipment manufacturers take the player's side
They give players the ability to give the ball a ride
Course designers take the PGA's side
They give the PGA the ability to stymie the player's pride

Extra length equals extra costs and green fees climb
Public pays the price, yet committed no crime
They are the champions of golf world lore
We are the losers of the golf world war

A double cross swing
Practice whiff or mulligan
Airmailing the green

Women's British Open 2012— Washing a Round

Officials deem second round null and void
This was a headline in a British tabloid
Sixty mph gusts created adverse conditions
An extreme wind that forced all decisions

Players stood braced as their ball blew from the tee
After three holes the officials invoked rule 33-2d
Marking a putt, then remarking became banal
It's no wonder they agreed it was unplayable

That morning produced quintuples on the scorecard
Cleansing yourself of that would not be hard
As easy as washing that round out of your hair
But I'm not so sure if that was fair

Eating the score is part of the game
It becomes a part of your fame not your shame
Both bad and good luck get washed down the drain
From pre-wash co-leader to 47th just ask Haeji Kane

Leaning on the hole
Had the grain for a sandy
Kiss me or kick me

World Challenge 2012— What Time Is It?

First week of the putter anchor ban had controversy
It unleashed USGA Mike Davis' fury
He called gallery criticism of Keegan's putter "unfounded"
I disagree, it's Davis' view that is not grounded

The gallery heckles of "cheater" he hated
Davis interpreted them as "uneducated"
USGA letter of the law was not created in a vacuum
Does he really think it started in his boardroom?

The basis of USGA law is in the spirit of the law
His failure to recognise this is his flaw
Spirit of the law is shaped by social norm
This is the tee box of USGA business platform

The golf cradle of the social norm is in the gallery
It is the gallery where putter criticism will get fiery
The problem lies in the bans transition of time
Spirit of the law can not tell time but it knows crime

Take care of your yips
Perfect speed for the back door
Whiskey a Go-Go

Rumour Has It

The golf course repair shack had a smell with a hefty kickback
A potion of grass, glue and gasoline that was less than serene
But this was unseen, otherwise the workshop was pristine
The clubhouse it was not, since it lacked any wainscot

A shack only in name, its exterior was held in high acclaim
A matchy matchy setting it mirrored the clubhouse trussing
"Say Mr. Lee your grip has finished drying," said the valet swinging
The young valet's duties included club washing and re-gripping

The country club member was known as the Asian Sensation
"I guarantee you'll dazzle the gallery with your short game."
Mr. Lee said, "Well then if I lose my aim I know who to blame."
The PGA pro took the wedge and considered the kid's pledge

"Thanks kid last minute decision, I really wanted to try this version."
The PGA pro held the grip up positioning it in the light
He then gripped it tight before declaring his delight
"They changed the bottom hand rubber, it needs less pressure"

Mind body and hole
Magical experience
Tee high let it fly

The valet knowing of the pros suspension had one question
"Say Mr. Lee when is the PGA planning on letting you play?"
Mr. Lee addressed the valet, held up the wedge and said, "Thursday"
"But everyone is saying you are suspended," the valet added

"Oh big big confusion, I'm not pothead I like my bourbon"
"But the TV, the papers, the PGA they all said you did not pass"
"Like I said, the lab run by big jackass, I really got a pass"
Mr. Lee fumbled with a pocket of his coat, while clearing his throat

"I got it all right here," he said holding the envelope saving his career
Mr. Lee vented by snapping the envelope on top of the workbench vise
"I go and got tested twice, the first obviously was not very concise"
"I got doctor letter, lab letter, PGA letter," said Mr. Lee holding his temper

"But Mr. Lee the rumours are widespread that you are a pothead"
"No no no cheap screening test I got cleared by a confirmatory test"
"After my protest they found that it was the pills I take to help me digest"
"No no no I am not pothead," said Mr. Lee as he tapped his head

Blisters and Band-Aids
Vardon overlapping grip
Watch away play last

"Just rumours kid I'll be on TV Sunday," Mr. Lee tucked his letters away
"I'm sorry we were all so sure you were suspended," he offered a hand
The pro shook his hand and said, "All is not true on the newsstand"
The pro peeled off a bill from his roll, "Thanks kid I'll chip it to the hole"

"Bye bye," said the gardener eating her lunch while sitting on a mower
"Where are you playing this week?" she said waving while holding a wafer
"In in in Canada over the border, a tournament where I'm a previous
winner"
Mr. Lee held his re-gripped wedge over his head high, while he said
goodbye

Sally thought some tact was required, "Someday Mordecai you will
get fired"
"You can't ambush the members with accusations for your amusement"
"You know me Sally and you know my schtick," went the valet's logic
"They all love me and all get chatty, they can't wait to tell me another story"

Sally hummed and hawed but refused to acknowledge him with a nod
"I think that you were mean to him, you should be more mindful,"
said Sally
"Sally Sally Sally Mr. Lee will seek me out Monday," said the valet suavely
"He knows that I know which keeps him needing to know how much I know"

Sunspots on your back
Achtung baby one roll short
Hot bothered and cool

"So he will be back that's why they all come back," he said tidying
    the shack
"I don't appreciate why you felt compelled to be Mr. Lee's contrarian"
"Say Sally hold it right there," the valet began, "You believed that man?"
"Oy vey, next you will be telling me that he is not wearing a toupee"

The valet leaned up against the workbench and fiddled with a cleat wrench
Sally ended her meal, moved the mower seat and pulled a knee to an armpit
"Let me tell you the story as I know it," Mordecai motioned claiming
    it legit
In his hands he gave the wrench a twirl as he addressed the pretty girl

"Did you notice despite it being daylight he held the club up to the light?"
"You are starting silly since he was wearing sunglasses," said Sally
"Precisely," said Mordecai. "That is my point exactly"
"Old-timers who have been here for decades, have only seen his shades"

"Our Mr. Lee appears to be a fashionista, who likes his hookah"
"Rumour has it he came from the old country with this calamity"
Sally sipped her coffee as she listened to the Asian Sensation story
Sally then remembered his problem, "I've been told this, it is gruesome"

Below the hole look
Barrel it straight it will die
Shot in to the heart

"You know about his girlfriend?" he thought his story was about to end
"No, don't shock me with some schmaltz. You have sources in China?"
"I have mensch from here to Asia," said Mordecai who then gulped
    his cola
"But Sally let me finish, I can't get to the reason for his sunglass fetish"

"It's rhetorical Sally, do you really think the hotshot doesn't smoke pot?"
"My read is, he may have acid reflux but really most days he smells rank
"Rumour has it, it's the pain he has to thank, he smokes a lot to be frank"
"He's got one eye that's crossed, he is lucky that it was not lost"

"Long ago before Ellen Woods, Mr. Lee sold his girlfriend a bill of goods"
"With lipstick on his lapel, his Asian sweetie delivered more than a
    lecture"
"A swing hell bent for leather and a nine iron that could not be straighter"
"She scored a crossed left eye and a single's life as a stoner with a stutter"

"Sally tell me I'm wrong but I won't be dating in Hong Kong"
"Given the consequences I say she used a three dressed up as a nine"
"I'm told via my grapevine, he has a steel plate just under the hairline"
"That Sally explains his shades and toupee," said the valet

Soft spikes and soft course
Driving rain heavy drivers
Showered card with pars

"Oh poor Mr. Lee, but Mordecai I heard the club gossip differently"
She continued, "Consider this when you choose to schmooze"
The valet smiled at the news and placed on the bench a pair of shoes
"A tale from the mysterious Far East," referring to the nearly deceased

"I heard this from the guys in cart maintenance, just by chance"
"From the start he was a superstar, all was his for the asking"
Mordecai kept smiling, he was all ears for a tale worth telling
"But I doubt he asked for a bong," speaking of his time in Hong Kong

Mordecai threw his hands in the air, instead of telling her of her err
Miffed at the valet's insolence she stated a grievance
She had lost all patience and shook a finger at his silence
"His plate is titanium not steel. Mind your sources they're not ideal"

Her face now red she said, "I believe that he is not a pothead"
Mordecai moved closer to the mower in order to change her mood
It wasn't his intent to start a feud, "Sorry Sally for being rude"
Sally placed a hand on the roll bar, "Ok let me tell you about his scar"

Can not hear it drop
Mind your clock pace of play rule
Within the leather

"Similar to your story the best player in China, ended up in a coma"
"Like your story he had a severe mishap consisting of a steel club shaft"
"A hazard of the craft," said Mordecai who then felt a draft
The scent of lilac, overwhelmed the shack

Through the door came a stylish woman full of pep and brisk of step
Her picturesque form was prim and polished, but was known as a poser
"Say Mrs. Stein how's my favourite club member?" he said with laughter
Mrs. Stein did not pause, "Sweetie have you finished my cougar claws?"

"Your cleats lack glamour, but you can now claim to be a cat scratch
    golfer"
"Mordecai you really work on your reputation," said Mrs. Stein with
    a smirk
The valet considered talking to the members a perk, never as work
She inspected the bottom of each shoe and said, "Did I interrupt you?"

He motioned to the mower, "Sally was telling me about a young Mr. Lee"
"Goodness, what has that nefarious numbskull been caught doing now?"
Sally fidgeted and smoothed her brow, "It's not important somehow"
Mrs. Stein answered, "Come on sweetie tell me what you have heard"

Peeking deciding
Should I stay or should I go
Putter to the sky

Sally was so furious with Mordecai she wanted to run out and cry
Conversely she vowed to vitiate the valet with vim and vigour
But neither were the answer, she would instead use candor
"Mrs. Stein your time is precious so I'll keep it short," was her retort

"He had the governor on his golf cart removed, an action not approved"
"The vehicular vandalism resulting in a high-speed crash, inevitable"
The valet heard a grumble but showed his approval by slapping the table
The member was not amused but the table slap kept her defused

"A broken steel golf shaft pierced his skull, the effect dreadful"
"Mr. Lee survived the surgery and lives with significant obstacles"
Mordecai whistles and tells Sally, "That's one for the annals"
The look on the face of Mrs. Stein indicated all was not fine

"Oh sweetie that's a twist on an old one, the bludgeon"
"I am always astonished in the diverse ways Mr. Lee gets the shaft"
"Excuse me if I laughed, what was that club number, this is getting daft"
Mordecai thought this was too good by half and continued to laugh

Letting the shaft out
Fairway rough or sand
Ball encased in ice

"Say Mrs. Stein over the years is it a nine iron that always appears?"
"Not always, rumour has it there was a rare medical reaction"
Sally thought Mrs. Stein was a bit of a bully and Mordecai a bit nervy
She gave the valet the hairy eyeball before listening to the worn doll

"For years I've wanted to get rid of Mr. Lee, that man has always
    upset me"
"First it was how he dressed then his dreaded guests now it's the drugs"
"I despise his faux kisses and hugs and even his phoney hair plugs"
"Thanks to the PGA he is finished, soon I will have him banished"

"He was just here saying goodbye, he has been reinstated," said Mordecai
Mrs. Stein became pensive, her blonde pony fixed on pause
Her review of all the club bylaws was now a lost cause
"Shabbadios," said Mrs. Stein, as she turned to the door and the sunshine

"Mrs. Stein, Mrs. Stein, please one more minute of your time"
"I relish your retrospection, give me something for a Mordecai revision"
She stopped and turned for that reason, she wanted history rewritten
"Rumour has it Mordecai, he was born that way," was her reply

Larvae cradle still
Iron horse views mid-iron stroke
No itching today

"I heard this from someone well-heeled in the medical field"
"She was a consistent source, don't say you heard it from me this time"
"Why past tense Mrs. Stein has she been convicted of a crime?"
"Bless her heart she has passed on," she said of her friend from Tucson

"You've heard of clubfoot," she said "Well this is called clubhead"
The valet looked down his nose, the gardener finished a sigh
"Now my young gadfly before you start consider that for his cockeye"
"It's a blood disorder that requires him to wear a visor"

"You are pulling my leg aren't you, a story that is not even on the menu"
She wanted him to run with the story, even say Lee got it in a restaurant
"Do with it what you want, it is yours to flaunt"
Mrs. Stein held up her shoes, "Thanks once more," and was out the door

"Oh Mordecai making me tell my story was just tacky," said Sally
"I was embarrassed, mortified but amused in the last minute"
The valet said, "In the last minute she was a real taffy pocket"
"You know me Sally it's all a game until the lawyers call my name"

Mighty lash in flight
Grand greens in regulation
Eye of the needle

Mr. Lee wiped his clammy skin after completing the airport bag
    check-in
For Mr. Lee the post-911 airport process produced plenty of stress
He practiced saying 'yes' as he waited for the customs line to progress
He would tell them he was a previous winner, everyone likes a winner

While practicing he saw the K9 unit, in an instant he felt like a magnet
The canine was getting close but he clutched his letters closer
His letter exonerating him as a doper did not make him feel any safer
As he talked to a customs official, the K9 unit hustled by on a schedule

From one line to the next he felt like he was on a conveyor belt
The twisting and turning and being compelled to talk made his head
    throb
Most were a humourless lot on the job, except the lady who took his swab
Hand to hand she said she was a fan, while he starred at the full body scan

The scanner was not like the old gizmo that chirped like a broken radio
It was a silent photo box as it accomplished it's digital strip search survey
He placed all things metal into a tray, as he prepared to enter the array
With feet wide apart and his hands over head it was a moment he dread

Ball core compression
Preferred lies lift clean and place
Over palms and moon

Passport and precious letters in hand he was prepared to be scanned
Squinting in the light Mr. Lee handed his letters to a man with a lanyard
Security read the letter saying he was not barred then he stared hard
With a crooked forefinger he made a jab at the letter from the lab

There was a note at the bottom, that airport security found irksome
"High iron levels consistent with a neurological condition," it said
"Colloquially known as clubhead," he read then reread
"A pro golfer with clubhead, really, enough said, go ahead"

The End

Launching the big dog
Trajectory unknown
Wagging the dog's tail

Acrostics

2012 Men's World Ranking Number One, Rory McIlroy

Received the Member of the Order of the British Empire proudly
Order of Merit winner on the European Tour, which is all about money
Ryder Cup team winner, which is all about the champagne
Year-end voting for PGA Tour Player of the Year, the start of his reign
Money winner on the PGA Tour was never in doubt
Cue European Tour Golfer of the Year whom the writers voted in a rout
In the end based on points he won PGA Player of the Year while the
    crowd roared
Lauded by the PGA Tour he then took the Byron Nelson Award
Received from the PGA of America the Vardon Trophy for scoring average
Outstanding win at PGA Championship sent Nicklaus a major message
Young Rory has become golf's favourite son after his rise to World
    Number One

Sighting hair fir tree
Big blue yonder distance rocks
Ball-crushing phenom

2012 Men's World Ranking Number Two, Luke Donald

Lovely rhythmic swing
Uses Odyssey when putting
King of the two-putt
Earned tour card by rarely missing a cut
Debut as pro the 2001 Reno Tahoe Open
Ongoing member of Ryder Cup a given
No major on his résumé
At home around the green his forté
Life membership on the European Tour
Destined for a Number One encore

Punching out of jail
Hit lumber on to green
Whole lotta carry

2012 Men's World Ranking Number Three, Tiger Woods

T is for towering approach shots
I is for innovation when in tight spots
G is for Grand Slam
E is for Electronic Arts video cam
R is for red shirt
W is for winning effort
O is for operating the Tiger Woods Foundation
O is for optimal swing motion
D is for driving the ball longer
S is for sensational golfer

Tag it off the tee
Tight fairway running away
Playing for some hay

2012 Men's World Ranking Number Four, Justin Rose

Johannesburg, South Africa, his city of birth
Usual residence a different place on earth
Stateside he lives in Florida on Lake Nona
Team Europe Ryder Cup member who plays with drama
Interests include sustainable golf facilities
Natural birdies are as important as scorecard birdies
Rated number one in greens in regulation
Often drives the ball without caution
Sand saves, he is ranked fourth at the beach
Embrace his play number one is not out of reach

Reservation Shade
Porch front store front bilge pump balls
Shag bag good and full

2012 Men's World Ranking Number Five, Adam Scott

Australian born and raised with down under mystique
Dialed in for ace during Masters Week
Amateur golf finishing school in Vegas
Managed obtaining Tiger's caddie with class
Secured a four shot lead for the Open's final round
Collapse during home stretch was profound
Open's final four holes all bogeyed
Title was trashed, burned and buried
Top World Five ranking showed he got stirred but not shaken

Bet the sucker pin
Laughing inside drives and chips
Mind your mental coach

2012 Women's World Ranking Number One, Yani Tseng

Y is for youngest player to win five majors, she was hot
A is for Annika's trophy case which Yani bought
N is for No, as in "No she can not swim"
I is for indeed she is the best golfer from the Pacific Rim
T is for Taiwan her birthplace
S is for the smile on her face
E is for "Egad! Have you seen how far that ball was driven?"
N is for no, as in "No, she will not become a Chinese citizen"
G is for great game, my highest acclaim

False front deception
A two stroke valley not seen
More club one less ball

2012 Women's World Ranking Number Two, Na Yeon Choi

N is for never in short sleeves
A is for the applause she receives
Y is for yardage she hits
E is for eagle scores she submits
O is for ominous stare that is Tiger-esque icy
N is for nickname NYC
C is for consistent putter
H is for her place as a Seoul Sister
O is for owning the US Open
I is for inevitable she will become World Number One

Robotic test swing
Pin seeker technology
Have you checked the hole

2012 Women's World Ranking Number Three, Stacy Lewis

S is for swimming in Poppie's Pond
T is for being terrific with the putting wand
A is for Amy Alcott and the pond tradition
C is for cuts made becoming certain
Y is for year-end leader with rounds in the sixties
L is for leading in eagles and birdies
E is for engaging character that makes us cheer
W is for winning the player of the year
I is for inward nine and the game on the line
S is for a swing that is subliminal by home design

Can't believe my eyes
Slippery left to right putt
Niagara Falls stunt

2012 Women's World Ranking Number Four, Inbee Park

I is for international winner
N is for Nevada where she schooled as an amateur
B is for bagging this year's money title
E is for entertaining win at Evian
P is for putting average leader in this one-year span
A is for lowest scoring average and the Vare Trophy
R is for ripping it long artfully
K is for knee-knocker, a day in the park for this golfer

Cross-hatched cut fairway
Jet stream sea breeze from Japan
Mustache-lipped bunker

2012 Women's World Ranking Number Five, Shanshan Feng

S is for shiny star from China
H is for hoisting LPGA Championship trophy to the strata
A is for aka Jenny
N is for nary a niblick when her nine-iron is just as lofty
S is for such a nice name it is said twice
H is for heeding her father's advice
A is for being an Asian sensation
N is for never being out of fashion
F is for being the first player from China on the LPGA
E is for encouraging others with her fine play
N is for notching wins on the international scene
G is for golf star like we have never seen

The KP is wild
Bit off plenty of the hole
Tiger in your tank

Scratch Eddie Loves Porgy

The question is always the same: "How did you get your nickname?"
They say shouldn't you be Bess, a bias belief at best
I protest and say the name is gender neutral in the Southwest
Besides I'm not disabled or black, I'm a tall, fit, lily-white Slovak

I've seen the Broadway production and felt its racial tension
It's Gershwin's classic compositions that carry me today
"Summertime" is a mainstay, but it's not my favourite I say
The Porgy and Bess soundtrack is simply a delicious snack

I chime, I'm named after the song if I don't have time
If I have time I tell them who tagged me with Porgy
Scratch Eddie named me after the song, "I loves you, Porgy"
He claims he is not a scratch golfer, go figure

Until today I've never said why Eddie named me Porgy
Or to the point of how the hustler came about to hang the moniker
It's a story of winning the heart of a hardcore bettor and golfer
Basically I'm a fast learner and in the dating world a better player

Hook into the trees
The woodpecker goes to work
Save par for barker

Scratch Eddie and I tied the knot five years ago at this very spot
This time capsule of a table that Eddie terms as his golf temple
But before it was a bridal table it was and still is his gaming table
This restaurant table for eight also was the place for our first date

I was a Vegas showgirl with a head of hair that would not curl
Scratch Eddie was an ostensive older olive-skinned suitor
Can't say he looked much like a golfer, thought he was a bowler
He didn't have that look Palmer made iconic, think Hitchcock

Our first date was here sampling the cuisine overlooking eighteen
Brunch with the burly man burst when I asked if he wore breeches
He was a Broadway whiz and we mostly talked about showbiz
He may not have looked like Arnold Palmer but was much calmer

For me it was love at first sight, then in walked a last minute invite
He was a tall, grey, gaunt golfer who had a ghastly pall to his wrinkled skin
He had the walk of a man about to sin but Eddie met him with a grin
"Your four chocolate chips as requested," then all talk halted

Left hand low pin high
Take a stand and ground your club
Power through the break

Casino chips stacked on the table, a result from the morning's battle
Scratch Eddie did not move a muscle much to the man's chagrin
The man stared at a napkin as if willing it to wipe Scratch Eddies grin
The silence continued, while the grey wrinkled man stewed

The man now fit to be tied, exited with what was left of his pride
Shocked by the silence but also how I did not summon a glance
Looking at the chips in a trance, I said I only charged ten cents a dance
My big boy lifted a smile and said the man would be back in a while

I say the silence made me uncomfortable, Eddie says it's artful
He went on with the secret to his success was not having the final say
"It's almost a cliché, before were finished he'll have something to say"
I ask if I should be afraid, Eddie says it's all a part of being played

He never said I should not be afraid but my interest did not fade
Curious about the circumstances of the chips I ask if they all pay
As if he consulted a mental dossier, there was a long delay
Eddie breaks the new silence and says with reverence, "Just once"

Sun shadows and sass
Dusk's double break dirt diver
Twisty yet bendy

"I hit pay dirt, before he died on the eighteenth with blood on his shirt"
I was appalled but his austere look and atonal words kept me speechless
Scratch Eddie was serious, but he exuded a warm world of softness
"The payout was over five million, he took it all to his coffin"

Before I can say who, he says it was some crazy Canuck corkscrew
A Canadian director for a failed American financial services firm
I got anxious and started to squirm, why, how, I wanted to confirm
Eddie says to settle in and sit tight and he would provide insight

His big brown eyes turn my stomach to jelly and he says Lacy
Lacy is not my natural name, no one in Vegas goes by their real name
I set my past aflame, I was going to be a Showgirl of high acclaim
Lacy he says it all started at this table, waiting for the payout haggle

The boys were listening to his talk of The Canuck's putting woes over tacos
He was a terrific striker, tight off the tee but terrible inside the leather
Given a four stroke buffer, which he flittered with each knee knocker
Hole after hole he was in the same position, his weakness was not hidden

Overnight drizzle
Greens fire reduced to embers
Slow cook the hot dogs

Eddie says keeping to script, in walked the crazy Canuck he had just
    whipped
He was skinny and seething, his short shiny black hair shone like a beacon
He stood in front of Eddie full of tension, a man intent on getting even
With Eddie sitting The Canuck standing, so began the next round of
    negotiating

"Your chocolate chips as requested," the casino chips clattered as they
    landed
A wad of bills hit the table with a thud, topped by a traditional cheque
The Canuck loosened a button at his neck, "I want to double up
    what's on deck"
As if releasing toxins he says he has conditions

Eddie says he sat as deadweight, waiting for The Canuck to show his bait
His lips unmoved his brown chips untouched, a potential payday unreal
The Pocket Tiger went into a spiel, "Conditions are no deal"
With Scratch Eddie silent, The Pocket Tiger passed judgment

Everyone Scratch Eddie knows gets a nickname, he does it without shame
The Pocket Tiger, best man at our wedding, also plays large in golf
    gambling
It goes without saying, he leaves a big game in his pocket while playing
The Pocket Tiger rose from the table, "From what I hear you are capable"

Mistaken ID
California Sea Lion
Call him Scratch Eddie

"You possess a golden short game, a few putts and the result is not
	the same"
"Eddie says you had one roll that snaked a path then slid in the side door"
The Pocket Tiger began to implore, "No conditions, handicap
	nothing more"
Eddie says the two of them continued to stand, he was silent as planned

The Canadian investment banker considered The Pocket Tiger
I'm told The Canuck was a cold ice hole who craved control
Eddie sensed their game had taken a toll, next he would take his bankroll
"You are right I think I've proven, I can play Eddie even"

"No strokes but I'm getting time and place, he will need a suitcase"
Once the word even escaped The Canuck's lips the endgame ensued
The Canuck had miscued, his conditions were only to improve his mood
"Tomorrow at my course in Canada, we continue this saga"

I'm told The Pocket Tiger countered with wanting to be Eddie's looper
The Canuck showed his distain and dismissed the last ditch dribble
I asked Eddie about the travel, it did not seem that this was usual
I thought this is where they would play ball, in the betting capitol

Crow's eye for the bag
Bike frame specification
Gleaming clubs and snaps

Eddie says once the strokes became even, The Canuck was beaten
He would go anywhere play anywhere agree to anything with the bettor
Chances of me asking and getting strokes go from laughter to never
But the setup is for the opponent to do something he shouldn't

Eddie says he assesses and praises his opponent's play all day
They began to realise that he is as right as a desert rain
What they see is insane, they see themselves in a scratch golfer's domain
Scratch Eddie is just a name, if they play even they will feel the pain

Eddie says the technique is flawless, they can beat his play they profess
It's a sickness even after losing they seek him out and surrender strokes
No arm twisting these folks, but sometimes they need a little coax
That's where The Pocket Tiger sings their song and helps steer them along

Eddie calls this helping to turn their ego in, or the setup to win
They all aspire to play scratch, a seduction to a mismatch
The Canuck had become a quite a catch, by giving four strokes in the
    rematch
The Canuck had money to burn, Eddie would take what he could earn

Chirping and pitching
Low with a roll to the hole
Kick in birdie

After The Pocket Tiger was refused as a caddie, Eddie spoke up gruffly
Eddie says securing money in the second game is always sublime
It is the crux of his livelihood at a time when he is in his prime
Now was not the time to be a pansy he wanted The Canuck's money

"Dusting off my passport is doubtful, unless the Nassau is pressing
this table"
"I also want an automatic no-limit, two-down press and an American
account"
"Oh my banker Canuck don't wince at the amount, there is no discount"
"Secure me the caddie services of your club's best amateur and I'm a flyer"

The Canuck agreed in his next breath, if he only knew it was his kiss
of death
Eddie says he flew on a private jet within the hour, and arrived fresh
as a flower
Business first as Eddie directed his chauffeur, to a restaurant for dinner
In the town of Banff he dined with an associate, a golf gambling summit

The next day Eddie was on the course at dawn whistling a Broadway song
The park setting he perused promised off fairway shots to be the worst
A ritual in which he was well versed, he visited the greens keeper first
He was suntanned with a Stimpmeter and hole cutter in each hand

Scoring high noon tea
Tasty fairway bomb and pitch
Peppering the flag

The greens keeper says, "You must be the guy, don't even try"
OK you put the pins in your position, his hands will still squeeze like
    a python
His chance gone, Eddie moved on to sand, seed and speed with the pawn
"They got the course closed this morning eh, you must be some hombre"

Eddie rode off in a cart, with the intent of confirming the yardage chart
Surrounded by a wilderness reserve the setting was stellar
Framed by a Rocky Mountain altar, Eddie expected golfing rapture
With 7,100 yards and a rating of 146 on the card, it was considered hard

After checking the chart and its angles, he found footing in one
    bunker's bowels
He spent an hour blasting his way out of the eighteenth bunker,
    bracing for battle
Eddie told me as usual, he retreated to the practice green ready to gamble
Eddie was holing putts while being served coffee and doughnuts

The Canuck arrived in his Range Rover, looking very much the golf
    warrior
Spiffy and full of polish with pinstriped pants presenting a perfect image
Emerging from The Canuck's entourage, a small and slight fella with
    a message
The member of the Cree Nation pointed at his chest and said, "Greysun"

Jumpsuits to rain suits
Face like a trodden bunker
Candies for caddie

The Canuck went to the driving range, Eddie found talking to
    Greysun strange
He didn't mumble anything more let alone if he could mind a bag
His shoulders looked like they would sag, clubs would go from carry
    to drag
Eddie thought it showed, The Canuck had found him on the side of
    the road

Eddie decided The Canuck had given him a raw deal but he would
    not appeal
Instead he showed the Indian ball cleaning, club cleaning, divot clearing
Eddie would do his own yardage calculating and his own scoring
With The Canuck at the range, there was some important info to exchange

Eddie unzipped a lower bag pocket and showed Greysun his secret
The young man began to laugh and laugh leaving Eddie's thoughts in limbo
Eddie wanted in on the sideshow so he grabbed Greysun's elbow
The laughter came to a stop and Greysun asks, "Is that a movie prop?"

Eddie says he began to laugh and says, "Don't shoot yourself in the calf"
Happy that Greysun could speak English Eddie explained everything
"Guns can't get through border screening, I got this from a movie setting"
"A golf friend in the business, this was all he could get on short notice"

All flesh bumper rails
Watches to stitches intense
Good attempts gone wild

"A shiny bright Clint Eastwood replica forty-five, a piece to keep me alive"
Pondering if it worked Greysun then weighed in, "When it's this big
    does it matter?"
Eddie tells him it's his friend's personal shooter and it has a proper trigger
Eddie says he was soft spoken and had the darkest eyes even for an Indian

Greysun zipped up the pocket to the gun, making an effort to keep it hidden
Carts were not allowed for the game, a grand scheme to grind him down
Overweight Eddie was to have a big step-down during the showdown
The Canuck misjudged Eddie's stamina, which had a walk in the
    park mantra

Greysun slung the bag over both shoulders wearing a holey pair of sneakers
The Canuck took a few swings, a few putts, fewer chips and was finished
His swing was well burnished, over-practicing part of his game banished
Eddie opened up a new sleeve of balls and reviewed The Canuck's
    shortfalls

Eddie and Greysun waited on the first tee for The Canuck and his party
"Welcome to the Cree Golf and Country Club with the cut set at two"
Eddie sipped his brew while being introduced to the rest of the crew
Two fore caddies, one bag caddie, one scorer and he presumed one advisor

Left slice dogleg right
Balls green stripes blow in the wind
Hybrid to rescue

"Sorry the caddie doesn't have much to say, the course markets them
    that way"
Eddie tells The Canuck that the caddie has confided in him secrets of
    the course
There was no need for remorse and that Greysun was a great resource
The Canuck looked at Eddie like he was full of it, he knew Greysun
    as a half-wit

Eddie tossed his empty cup into a bear-proof bin, let the game begin
Enough with the warm up he would bring out the whip and win
This would not be a game filled with spin, it would be green light to
    the pin
Yesterday The Canuck didn't have the talent, why would today be
    different?

Eddie threw and won the tee toss, this should be considered in any
    loss
Eddie wins at everything even the tee toss has its own trick of the
    trade
Eddie with honours to start his crusade said he wouldn't give it up
    until he got paid
Eddie hit driver and right out of the gate showed what was in store
    for the banker

The Canuck and Eddie walked off the first tee, while Greysun stood
    under a tree
Eddie did not look but The Canuck bent behind his back making
    certain
"Is he talking to that raven?" "No he's checking the yardage book jargon"
Eddie then told him not to worry and thanked him for so fine a
    caddie

After the ball mark
Half ball wide then one ball wide
Afraid of the dark

The Canuck wanted to fire him for being strange, it was not too late
    to change
Eddie told him not to lose his mind in the moment, he's marketed
    that way
Eddie took pleasure in defending his caddie, he could be strange all day
With The Canuck being upset at the onset, this was considered an asset

After Eddie won the first two there was an automatic press and distress
The Canuck huddled his caddie and scorer with the advisor at the centre
The situation had become dire, as Scratch Eddie's game caught fire
Birdie birdie out of the gate was enough to make The Canuck vibrate

At the end of four there was another automatic press for more
I asked Eddie if The Canuck had played poorly, he says he was at par
The opening holes would leave a scar but it wasn't time for a cigar
Eddie took the Nassau's front nine, plus extra presses that were on the line

After nine there was score confirmation, The Canuck was down over
    a million
The Canuck conferenced with his team, concocting a plan for the course
Greysun stood apart from Eddie as in divorce, he wasn't much of a
    resource
Waiting for The Canuck at the turn, he was served fresh coffee from an urn

Gusty dilemma
Grip and rip or lay it up
An arched bridge too far

Checking the wind in the trees, he saw a raven that made him freeze
It seemed to be staring straight at Greysun and making a soft,
    clicking sound
Before restarting the round Eddie walked over to confirm what he
    had found
Pointing to the bird as black as coal, he asked if it followed them hole
    to hole

"Oh no Mr. Vegas the raven travels in a pair, a single would be rare"
"Greysun stop feeding the raven, next we will have a flock following"
Eddie says he heard the clicking change to a low guttural rattling
The oily plumage was noted, should this situation need to be tended

Like the front nine Greysun started the back nine lagging at the hole sign
For the tenth hole in a row The Canuck bent behind his back making
    certain
"Is he talking to that raven?" "No but start worrying if he feeds it carrion"
Still Eddie did not look back, but said he couldn't stop the wisecrack

The automatic press was not taken lightly, The Canuck went bogey-bogey
Eddie gave The Canuck some time to scour his scorecard for the
    money shot
Eddie expected a recovery press going for knot, creating a jackpot
While waiting for the expected gambling action he talked to Greysun

Staring down the shaft
Trust putter alignment line
Let the thunder roll

"I'm just curious Greysun, are you talking to that raven?"
Eddie had to confess, a crooked line was crossed with an answer of 'yes'
"The raven said someone is going to die in the excess of the final press"
He grabbed the scrawny Cree Indian's shirt in an outburst, shook
    him and cursed

"The Canuck asks did I interrupt something, did you catch him stealing?"
"Listen Eddie pass on the little prick, I'm double pressing you on
    eighteen for everything"
The Canuck saw the sweat running down Eddie's brow and left laughing
Eddie figured The Canuck was the source of this flap, and then
    Greysun spoke up

"Mr. Vegas it is the banker who is going to die," he says going from
    enemy to ally
Greysun lifted the line-illustrated yardage book up to Eddie lending
    his proof of life
"The banker's approach to these tombstones and wildlife behind
    eighteen will be full of strife"
Eddie thought the hand drawn illustration for a graveyard was easy
    to discard

"Accept his press then go for more he doesn't know what is in store"
Eddie put his sweaty hands around his caddie's neck squeezing and
    swearing
The Canuck put him up to this, Eddie was yelling when the ravens
    began cawing
The trees were chock-a-block with the coarse and abrasive call of a flock

A sign from above
Flagstick shadow is your guide
Stroke it down the line

Greysun replied before the aerial attack, "They're on our side"
He let go of Greysun's frail neck to protect his face from the frenzied ravens
With few options, he thought he was going to die in those mountains
Gunfire erupted over his head, he looked up thankful he was not dead

The ravens retreated to the wilderness with speed, leaving Eddie bloodied
The Canuck stood over them with a gun, "Our Good Grace it's not
    garbage day"
"You two get up I saved you from the buffet, we've got one more hole
    to play"
Before Eddie could get towelled off The Canuck demanded that he
    say yes to his press

Eddie looked at Greysun and accepted the press but would ignore the
    push for more
He dabbed at a few of the deeper scratches and dusted dirt off his shirt
Greysun appeared to be unhurt as he once again stood back looking alert
Eddie put his ball cap back on and contemplated a bigger con

The par four eighteenth pin was four-thirty, Eddie figured three
    strokes to glory
"My banker Canuck I didn't know guns were criteria for this course"
"Of course in this case I can endorse the show of force"
"Now for a little candor what does your scorekeeper say that we are
    playing for?"

Address with head down
Ants from ankle to waggle
Whiff shot or kill shot

Eddie agreed with the math but didn't like the basis of the smugness
Were the tells in the threat of death, soiled trousers or his torn shirt?
Eddie was alert to The Canuck's high level of comfort
After two games of losing he still thought he could go from zero to hero

Both tee shots from eighteen were in play, in the heart of the fairway
According to Greysun The Canuck's approach was going gorge-side
    in the graveyard
Instead he hit it tight showing he would die hard, if he put a birdie
    on the card
Eddie said at that point he viewed his Indian caddie suspiciously

Was he in The Canuck's employ as part of a physiological ploy?
Eddie bore down knowing he needed his ball to bite but got backspin
    and bunker
Eddie said it could not have rolled in any gentler, position B for the gambler
Knowing the bunker position was fine he studied the roll line

I asked what was Greysun up to, he said, he was off green, quiet like
    a homemade tattoo
Scratch Eddie picked a club with big bounce and blasted the ball out
    of the bunker
The ball came out with a fine sand trailer, its landing and roll leaving
    little to wonder
With two days of bet pressing on the line Eddie shaped a sandie for birdie

Magnetic marker
Edge heart or apex of break
Firm stroke for good roll

The Canuck did not flinch, he was studying his two-foot Scott
Choch down to the inch
The banker needed the putt to push the game, he stood back
pondering his aim
Eddie in a move intending to inflame, marked The Canuck's ball
then made a claim
"My banker Canuck you think I'm not wise to Greysun and Titanic
Thompson?"

He bent over the hole in the dirt and pulled out the top-half of the
metallic hole insert
Eddie moved the magnetised ring over The Canuck's ball snapping
metal to metal
The ball and ring were thrown Molotov-style into the graveyard
without quarrel
"You have missed every putt inside the leather, place a new ball, the
bet is it won't fall"

The Canuck's scorekeeper piped up, "All games" Eddie replied, "All games"
Fore caddies, bag caddie, scorekeeper, advisor conferenced in panic
Greysun remained stoic and static as he tended the pulled flagstick
Eddie noted the position of his golf bag that was near the flag

The Canuck gave a confident stroke to his putt, only to see it horseshoe out
There were muted murmurs as The Canuck put his hand to his
mouth after he missed
Greysun pulled a flat black gun from under his vest and shot The
Canuck in the chest
"Thank you Vegas the bullet was for my tribes honor, but I wanted to
see him die a loser"

Flight confirmation
Par took migratory route
Birdie gone deep south

The Canuck's entourage scattered after the malice, Greysun slipped
    into the wilderness
"Lacy it was like I was at death's door as ravens descended adding to
    the despair"
"Dead men with nine pair of raven picking at their hair don't pay
    their share"
"So do they all pay? Not all, just this once, when I got caught up in
    tribe vengeance"

I remember being in a mesmerized state, this was after all our first date
Millions in money, murder, mayhem and a master manipulator at the centre
I took it all in every whisper, I always considered myself a good learner
I wondered what caused the vengeance so I asked what was the tribe's
    grievance

Eddie says Greysun has never been found to this day but this is what
    the RCMP say
The tribe was busted and broke after dealing with The Canuck's US
    investment bank
All hope sank, when the SEC didn't believe it could win in court
    with the bank
The RCMP have little doubt that this is a result from the subprime fallout

Eddie was going to continue when he was interrupted mid-remark by
    that morning's mark
The tall, grey, gaunt golfer with a ghastly pall to his wrinkled skin
    had something to say
Eddie clammed up as is his play but when the old man stammered I
    joined the foray
"Eddie says you possess a golden short game, a few putts and the
    result is not the same"

Roll outside the roost
Delicate one coming back
Cock-a-doodle-doo

Leaning far forward I got the old man's attention, adding sexuality to
    the tension
"I hear you had one roll that snaked a path then slid in the side door"
Before lunch he treated me like a part of the décor but now I was
    playing hardcore
"I've made a tee time for tomorrow and you are right I'll shave a
    stroke to make it so"

The old man turned and left to go practice his golfing while Eddie
    was left beaming
I say, "So did I sing his song and help steer him along believing he
    could beat Scratch Eddie?
Did I just score a stack of money, or do you think of me as some
    dumb dame floozy?"
A Broadway tune could be heard playing softly and Eddie says, "I
    loves you, Porgy"

The End

Balloon in the wind
Cabbage ball reach for the knife
Let the divot fly